THE BIGFOOT OF CEDAR RIDGE

The Adventures of Bog

(Book One)

Foot Print

Fiasco

by

Robert Rogers

Suzzanna Ravenlight, editor/artwork

I

Published by Squatchcamp Press

ISBN 978-1-969768-03-3 (paperback)

First edition: 2025

Permissions/contact: squatchcamppress@gmail.com

Table of Contents
The Bigfoot of Cedar Ridge
The Adventures of Bog
"Foot Print Fiasco"

"You're berry-drunk, Piney," Bog grinned.

Chapter One

"The Muddy Caper"

The soft beam of the hiker's headlamp bobbed back and forth across the trail like a confused firefly as he traversed the rugged terrain. It was nearly dusk, and the woodsy silence was interrupted, if ever so briefly.

Thwack.

A small acorn pinged off the man's backpack, barely causing the hiker to look up.

"Squirrels," he mumbled under his breath.

He kept climbing the rocky trail, eyes focused directly in front of him so he wouldn't trip. His walking stick tapped out an irregular tempo each time it connected with the ground.

Thwack.

This time, the impact was more forceful. A pine cone bounced off the man's shoulder and rattled down the slope through the dry leaves.

"Hey," he shouted. "What the—what in the hickory nut is going on here?"

The young hiker stopped and raised his head, causing the weak beam of light attached to his hat to momentarily rise and focus on the trail in front of him.

The sun had already ducked below the horizon, causing familiar shapes to look—well, ghostly. He looked ahead, his light catching the switchback sign and crooked slope. No one else around.

A rustle in the canopy close by caught his attention. He squinted toward the sound, as if the trees owed him an apology.

Then, silence.

Up in the pine, two bright eyes blinked. Bog slid behind the thick trunk and went perfectly still. Stillness was his family specialty, Bigfoots had practiced it for generations.

Shimmer. Breathe. Vanish.

His accomplice, Pinecone, Piney to friends, was an entirely different story. Piney did not do stillness. The fox squirrel buzzed with mischief and loved a good hiker heckle.

He was fiercely loyal to Bog, and the two were inseparable. He narrated everything in short, snappy bursts, like a sportscaster.

"Aaaand he delivers the pitch," the squirrel whispered into Bog's ear.

With that announcement, Piney leapt from Bog's shoulder, crashed through a pine branch, and tumbled into the needles below. Chittering—which sounded like laughing—he righted himself and scurried noisily through the leaves.

Below, the hiker watched the commotion, a thin smile of relief creeping across his face. He let out a sigh and started up the trail again. It was only a short hike back to the campground, and the darkness was beginning to close in and give him that weird feeling he was being watched.

Bog—Bogden, when his parents were mad, was a thirteen-year-old Bigfoot with a snack-sniffing nose and feet like furry snowshoes. Big heart. Bigger curiosity. Without Piney, he'd be in way more trouble.

The evening breeze shifted, and Bog's nose began twitching involuntarily. Someone nearby had marshmallows. Curiosity nudged him forward—exactly the habit that got him in trouble. Good thing Piney was close by.

The lone hiker finally moved far enough in the distance for Bog to breathe a sigh of relief.

"Close one," the squirrel chittered. "Almost struck out."

Piney scrambled up the trunk as Bog set both giant feet on the ground with a soft thud.

"That was exciting," Bog said, catching his breath.

The squirrel jumped onto his friend's shoulder, and the two struck off on another adventure. This time, Bog's nose was doing the driving.

"Marshmallows," Bog whispered. "Soft, sugary, vanilla, ooey-gooey goodness."

"Foul ball. No good, no good," Piney chittered.

"You love marshmallows, Piney," Bog said, smacking his lips as if to prove how tasty marshmallows were.

"I do, I do," Piney chittered, "but the smell is coming from the campground."

"Stranger danger. Too many humans."

It was too late. Bog was drawn to the sugary smell like a tractor beam. Walking slowly, he stepped where the shadows lived in silence and the pine needles were softest, which was difficult because his feet were neither silent nor soft.

They were enormous, like two shaggy sleds. They made soft squishing noises that sounded, unfortunately, like, I was here, I was here.

Reaching the far edge of the campground, the duo stopped. For long minutes, they remained motionless, their outlines camouflaged among the trees and brush.

Sniff, sniff.

They were close to the sweet snacks—too close for Piney. The two stayed hidden as the last remnants of daylight escaped to wherever daylight escapes.

"Chancy play," Piney whispered. "You'll never make it."

"Don't worry," Bog said, almost under his breath. "I'm sneaky."

But Bog was not sneaky. He was careful, which is different. And he was kind, which is harder to pull off for a Bigfoot.

With his sidekick firmly riding his shoulder, Bog slipped between two tents, brushing past a picnic table toward the sweet smell of white, fluffy marshmallow heaven.

All of a sudden, his heel sank into something cold and sticky. Mud. Fresh, dark, and perfect for capturing the shape of a foot. His foot.

"Abort mission, abort mission," Piney whispered. "You printed."

Bog slowly began to lift his foot.

The mud made a long sccchhhloooooooook as it tried to keep the giant furry foot. Holding his foot momentarily in the air, he stepped forward only to see another print form behind him.

Nothing was worse to a Bigfoot than leaving tracks that aroused human curiosity. It was a rookie mistake, and Bog knew it.

"What do we do, what do we do," Piney muttered, too flustered to think straight.

"It'll be fine," Bog said. "The mud will dry and smooth itself out."

"Before or after the humans follow our trail?" Piney quipped.

"They'll find us, all of us. We're doomed," the squirrel added, almost to himself.

"Stop it," Bog said. "I need to think."

"We'll sweep them away with a branch. That'll do it," Bog said. "First, the marshmallows."

A grocery bag dangled from a tree branch near the picnic table, tied up high—clever for raccoons, less clever for

Bigfoots. Bog reached up with his furry, human-like hand and pulled.

Crack.

At that the unmistakable sound of a zipper scraped open nearby. Click. A flashlight beam began to dance around the inside of one of the tents.

"Shhhh," Piney hissed.

Bog slowly and silently crouched, resembling a shrub more than a bipedal primate in the woods. Bigfoots had lots of tricks to avoid discovery, like sinking into their own shadow.

Bog's mind raced. The smell of marshmallows drifting up from the bag, combined with the knowledge that he had made a very loud mistake with his feet in the mud, sent his heart pounding.

Thump-thump. Thump-thump.

The seconds stretched into minutes—an eternity for the young Bigfoot and his companion. Bog's knees started to ache, and he shifted uncomfortably over his two massive feet.

Finally, the light beam drifted away. The zipper rasped shut. The tent went still.

Only then did they melt toward the relative safety of the tree line.

"Now?" Piney breathed.

"Now," Bog said.

They slipped between the tents once more. Bog untied the bag, fished out two fluffy white marshmallows, and handed one to Piney as he popped the other into his mouth. The pair savored the sugary confection as if it were the finest treasure ever found.

All the while, Bog could hear his Nana Moss in his thoughts. "The Bigfoot Code, Bogden. Leave no trace— nothing that leaves YOU behind." Nana Moss was a wise older Bigfoot, the keeper of the Bigfoot Code and master of moss tea and hideouts. She had a habit of looking over her glasses when she was displeased with Bog's adventures. She knew Bog as well as anyone, and also happened to be his grandmother.

"What about your titanic toe prints back there?" Piney said.

"Right," Bog said. "The footprints. We said we'd sweep them out with a branch."

He snapped off a fern frond from a nearby bush, and the two cautiously made their way back to the mud hole, careful not to step in the goo again. Using the fern, Bog swiped back and forth across the muddy track.

The mud smeared into a larger, messier shape that looked less like a foot and more like a monster that wore a foot as a hat.

"There," Bog whispered. "Is that better?"

"Worse," Piney said unapologetically. "It is definitely worse."

Bog bent to give the prints another swipe—then froze.

From the road, the rattling sound of a truck that had seen too many back roads broke the silence.

Squeak, squeak. Rattle-rattle. Vroom.

"It's Ranger Rudy!" Piney said. "He's coming for night rounds."

Ranger Rudy was a rule-following park ranger with a soft spot for animals, and he had always suspected "something" in Cedar Ridge.

"Escape, escape. Game over," Piney ordered, mustering his most authoritative voice.

Ducking slightly—as Bigfoots did when they walked—and with Piney latched firmly onto his shoulder, Bog receded into the woods.

The pair of mischievous mammals used the silhouettes of trees, rocks, and bushes to obscure their movement.

Leave no trace, Nana Moss's voice echoed in Bog's head. Leave no trace.

Chapter two

"Operation Mud Mix-Up"

Juniper "June" Reyes was enjoying the last tidbits of whatever adventure twelve-year-old vloggers dream about when voices outside her tent woke her.

Daylight was already washing the tent walls as she lay there, momentarily unsure whether the voices were real or leftovers from a dream.

Ugh, she thought as the voice continued.

It was unmistakably Jax Donovan—a prepubescent teen with a habit of getting into, or causing, trouble wherever he went. Everyone called him Jinx. It fit.

June unzipped her tent and crawled out—straight into Jinx's presence. He stood less than ten feet away, pointing at the ground, almost hysterical.

"L–look!" he stammered, dancing in place. "It's a—it's a—it's a Sasquatch track!"

He stared squarely at the mud hole. The same mud hole Bog had printed in the night before.

"You mean Bigfoot, you dolt," June said, in the most dismissive tone she could manage. "Sasquatch is a Native American name, of which you are most certainly not."

Jinx didn't hear the lesson. "This is huge," he breathed. "I'm gonna be famous."

June was not your average curly-haired preteen girl. She could ask a hawk for the weather, scold raccoons over stolen snacks, and give a deer directions—all before homeroom.

At twelve, she spent more time in the Cedar Ridge woods than anywhere else. Camera clicking and boots muddy; she was always on the lookout for honest adventure. She had two talents: talking to animals and finding trouble worth filming.

With her Bigfoot bestie, Bog, and his sidekick, Piney, she logged the Cedar Ridge woods like they were her backyard—which, if she was being honest, they practically were.

June peered down at the muddy footprint, and her stomach dropped.

"Bog," she whispered.

"What? What did you say?" Jinx smirked.

Thinking quickly—as she always did—June blurted, "Er, um, frogs. It must've been frogs."

Jinx snorted, clutching his belly as he laughed. "Frogs? That's the dumbest thing I've ever heard. Frogs."

"Shut up. You're dumb," she snarled. Not her best retort.

This is a disaster, she thought. I have to destroy these before somebody gets any bright idea about taking pictures. Or worse—casting them.

June squinted toward the trees, scanning for any sign that her bestie and his sidekick were nearby. Nothing. Then it came to her.

"You guard the tracks, Jinx, while I go get my camera."

I'll make sure these never make the news; she told herself.

She ducked into her tent and grabbed her camera bag.

"Batteries, batteries," she muttered. "Why didn't I change these already?"

She fumbled in the bag and plucked out two fresh batteries.

Without wasting time, she loaded the camera as she stepped back outside and headed toward the mud hole.

Too late.

Standing beside Jinx was a nightmare named Waldren—five feet six inches of cryptid confidence. He already had his phone out, snapping pics. He peered at June from under his safari hat.

"It always pays to be ready to document evidence," he said in his whiny, too-smug voice, gesturing at the mud hole.

He portrayed himself as the one who would finally prove the existence of Bigfoots at Cedar Ridge.

Pictures, June thought. This will be all over the internet in an hour. What a disaster.

It didn't take that long.

June knew Waldren's website all too well. He was a local "adventurer" and one of the biggest threats to Bigfoot secrecy.

She pulled up his site on her phone—affectionately named Waldren's Wacky World. A befitting name, she mused.

There, on the front page, a headline that could ruin it all: Bigfoot Terrorizes Campers at Local Campground.

There were only two things the curly-headed vlogger hated: peas and click bait. Especially the kind that drew attention to her furry friends in the forest.

I have to think of something quick, June thought. This place will be crawling with people soon. As long as someone doesn't call the ranger—

Squeak, squeak. Rattle-rattle. Vroom.

Ranger Rudy's old truck labored up the service road like a rusty beetle. June's heart kicked.

This just got worse.

As the ranger approached, Jinx windmilled both arms. "Rudy! You gotta see this!"

June swallowed. Think fast. She needed time, water, and friends with tails—and a story that didn't end with Bog on the front page.

Ranger Rudy parked, grabbed a small notepad and a roll of flagging tape from his dashboard, and headed toward the growing cluster of campers.

"Let's give this space, folks," he said.

He knelt and studied the print without sensationalizing; fingers braced at his chin. He asked who found it first. Jinx pointed at himself. Waldren waved his phone.

"Ummmm, could be bear tracks," June offered, a little too nervously.

"Could be, could be," Ranger Rudy said, drawing out the words as he thought. "Mud distorts." He paused. "But this one's... big."

Rudy was practical and methodical.

"Waldren, I'd appreciate it if you didn't post this until we've had a chance to investigate a little more."

"The public has a right to know," Waldren retorted, smugly raising his phone like a trophy.

Still kneeling, Rudy looked up at the onlookers, pausing on Waldren with an almost incriminating stare. "Of course, if this sparks a crowd, we'll have to close the trails."

The commotion drew another sort of crowd—the four-footed kind.

June heard the rapid, high-pitched chatter of Vex and Hex, twin raccoons: part-time thieves, full-time comedians. They were always nearby when adventure broke out.

Eureka, June thought. That's it. Vex and Hex can help.

She eased backward, slipping away from the group without anyone seeming to notice. One glance back confirmed that all eyes were still on the tracks—and the ranger.

At the edge of the campground, June pursed her lips and whistled. Two notes.

Immediately—squeak-squeak.

Zigzagging out of the trees, the rambunctious troublemakers scampered to her.

They couldn't stop moving—paws busy, noses busier, lifting every shiny object to their mouths.

The twins were hard to keep focused, even on a good day. Vex stooped to pick up something a camper had dropped and stuffed it in his pocket.

"Look, guys, we're in trouble. Big trouble," June said. "Jinx found one of Bog's prints, and now everyone knows."

Vex popped onto his hind legs and windmilled his little hands. "Let me at 'em! Let me at 'em!"

Hex, calmer, folded his hands like a tiny professor. "Destroy the tracks," he said.

"Exactly," June said. "We need those prints gone. Waldren already posted pics, but we can keep this from getting worse."

She straightened. "Commence Operation Mud Mix-Up."

Back at the mud hole, Ranger Rudy stood with his notepad, so focused he didn't notice June slip in beside him. He stared past the trees as if looking for something specific, tapping his pen against the cardboard backing.

"I should probably cast these," he said, mostly to himself.

Oh no, June thought. The last thing we need is permanent proof of the Bigfoot buzz.

Vex and Hex had already ghosted into position in the shadow of the nearest tent. Operation Mud Mix-Up had to work.

Ranger Rudy glanced at June. "I'll need to get some water and the plaster from the truck," he said, calm and steady, as if reassuring the onlookers that he had things under control.

Underneath the calm, his pulse was jumping. He had long suspected something unusual might be roaming the hills of Cedar Ridge. Could this be the proof the world was waiting for?

Excited or not, Rudy moved methodically. His boots squished as he headed for the service road.

Not about to lose credit or recognition to anyone, Waldren and Jinx trailed after him.

"I'll help," Waldren chirped.

"Don't forget I found the track," Jinx added.

Rudy looked up just enough to nod as the trio moved off toward the truck.

At least they can help carry gear, he thought.

June wasted no time. She caught the raccoons' eyes. "Ready?"

Vex and Hex were always ready, with the kind of nervous energy that could get anyone into trouble—or out of it.

"Go, go, go," June whispered.

Hex and Vex launched from the tent's shadow, chittering at full volume, and charged straight for the mud hole.

"Weeeeeee!" shouted the mud-bound maestros as their little clawed feet landed smack in the middle of the track.

They sprinted through the mud, skidded to a stop on the far side to squabble theatrically, then tore back along the same path.

"Oh no," June winced. "Your feet are so small, I don't know if it's working. Now it looks like a messy monster walking a pet raccoon."

The commotion drew attention fast. Ranger Rudy, Waldren, and Jinx sprinted back toward the mud hole. Jinx— the youngest and fastest—reached it a good ten steps ahead of the others.

"Get those raccoons out of there! They're ruining everything!" he screamed, his voice cracking with the strain.

June hopped back before he bowled her over.

Sometimes problems solve themselves.

Jinx was too busy saving the day to notice the tent stake.

"Aaaaaaa!"

He launched—an aero-teen for three glorious seconds—

Whump.

He covered the last few feet to the mud hole in midair, arms out like Superman, and face-planted into the sticky mud.

Ranger Rudy and Waldren arrived moments later, just in time to see Jinx lift his face from the muck. Mud masked him like a swamp creature more than a cryptid connoisseur.

"YOU," Waldren sputtered, throwing up his hands, "you've ruined the tracks!"

Ranger Rudy stood very still. A thin, almost satisfied smile tugged at his mouth. "You live to mystify again, my friend," he murmured, his eyes flicking toward the tree line.

Vex and Hex didn't stick around for the finale. They were already scurrying for the safety of the forest, ringed tails flagging behind them.

"Well, I guess that's that," June said, dusting off her hands.

"I still got pictures," Waldren snapped.

"Yeah—pictures of a mud hole," June said with a smirk, spinning toward her tent.

From the shadowed pines, Bog let out the breath he didn't know he'd been holding. On his shoulder, Piney chittered,

"Safe at home... for now," and the two melted back into the
woods.

Chapter Three

"Green Prints"

"BOGDEN!"

The name echoed through the hollow—soft and hard at the same time—the unmistakable mothering tone of Maple Fernfoot.

Bog jerked his head up from the stream where, moments before, he'd been studying his reflection for tiny flecks of marshmallow stuck in his fur.

On his shoulder, Piney began to quiver. "Your parents know. Game suspension," the squirrel whispered.

"Get home this instant, Bogden!" Maple's voice boomed to every nook and cranny of Shimmerleaf Hollow, where the Bigfoot clan made their home.

Bog knew any delay would make it worse. His shoulders drooped. Eyes on his feet more than the path, he and Piney hurried toward home—a cave tucked behind a thatch of brambles so thick no human could "accidentally" find it.

At the entrance, Bog spotted his mother by the table, hands planted on her hips.

"Have a seat, young man," she said, nodding at the chair.

"I was just—"

"I'll do the talking," Maple cut in, her eyes flashing.

News traveled fast in the forest. Every animal in Cedar Ridge depended on the others to keep them safe.

"A little birdie told me they found tracks at the campground," Maple said. "The kind of tracks a Bigfoot makes."

In this case, the birdie was a chickadee named Penny Ping—Penny for short. From the treetops, she could spot trouble long before anyone else.

Bog's shoulders crept lower. He stared at the floor.

"What were you doing in the campground, Bogden Fernfoot?"

"I—I was looking for some snacks... marshmallows," he mumbled.

"You and your snacks are going to get us all in trouble," Maple said, lifting her hands even higher on her hips.

She turned her gaze to the squirrel. Piney nearly slid off Bog's shoulder.

"And you? Where were you while this was happening?"

Piney opened his mouth, then quickly shut it.

"Eating a marshmallow, I suppose," Maple said.

Piney made no sound at all. He was terrified of Bog's parents when they were upset.

"Your father will hear about this when he gets back from the blackberry patch," Maple said. "I'll tell you that right now."

"You're grounded from the edge trails, Bogden. Do you understand me?"

"Yes, Mother," Bog said, shifting in the chair.

"We're going to have to do damage control. When the coast is clear, you and Piney will go back and make sure you erase all tracks around the campground and repair anything that might leave a clue."

She leaned closer. "You'll replace them with green prints that no one will suspect. Green prints are tracks from animals campers expect to see around campsites—deer, rabbits, opossums. Somehow, the humans find green prints comforting."

"Penny can watch from above, but first you'll visit Nana Moss. Nana has a mulch-camouflage trick that will keep you out of sight longer than a shimmer."

Maple's anger softened to worry, her eyes now more teary than the fire-breathing monster from moments ago.

"Look at me, Bogden. Not the floor. I am not angry at you for being you. You are curious, and that's a good thing when you carry it carefully. But our family lives by a code because curiosity leaves prints."

Penny fluttered in with a breathless update. "The campers are forming some kind of search party to look for more prints." Her tiny chest heaved. "Clock's ticking."

Maple pulled Bog into a quick hug. "Now, Bogden Fernfoot, go be smart."

Nana Moss lived about an acorn's throw from Bog. Good thing, too—he had spent most of his childhood there.

Nana was older, as evidenced by her soft gray hair. She was wise even beyond her years and, to Bog, softer than the other Bigfoots.

Bog and Piney had barely reached Nana's door before she blurted, "I already know what happened, Bog."

This was Nana Moss. She seemed to know things before things happened.

"I've already started the mulch we'll use for camouflage," she said, looking at Bog over her glasses, matter-of-fact.

She stepped close and laid her big, soft hand on his shoulder. Looking down through her glasses, she said, "You stepped where the mud remembers. So, we will remember better.

We don't hide because we're ashamed. We hide because the forest is small when crowds get big. Your size, your heart, your feet—they're gifts. Use them to cover, to carry, to care."

"Today you'll make green prints. You'll erase what shouldn't be seen, and you'll leave something kinder in its place."

"Piney, you'll keep his head up and his paws out of the marshmallows."

"When you come home, I want to hear not just what you fixed, but who you helped. That's how a Fernfoot walks."

She handed Bog a small bag of leaves. "Hold the bag firmly, and as you start to shimmer, you'll blend into the trees behind you without a trace."

"Before you go, have Penny do a flyover and make certain you know where everyone is."

"Piney, you be on the lookout for movement and metal. Anything shiny—glasses, phones, watches—belongs to humans, not Bigfoots."

"Remember, shimmer-blend; move downwind."

Even when it felt like a scolding, Bog knew Nana was looking out for him.

Bog and Piney struck off to undo what had been done. With luck, the green prints would work. Stopping only to fill a gourd flask with water and snap off a fresh fern frond, they headed toward the campground.

On the way, Bog noticed a log he'd kicked over with his big feet during the last foray. "Remember to undo what has been done, Bog." Nana Moss's advice echoed in his head. He righted the log to its original position. Part of the code.

Soon, the duo reached the edge of the campground. They crouched and waited, hidden, until night offered protection. As darkness settled, Penny flew over and issued a single chirp.

Single chirps meant all clear. Double chirps meant danger.

All the while, "the Code" ran through Bog's mind:

- Move slowly; use what's already there.

- Leave the place a little kinder than you found it.

- Don't trample nests, burrows, or plants.

- Don't escalate pranks that invite more humans.

- Chase the quiet, not the chaos.

- Backtrack on hard ground or rock.

- Pause twice to listen before crossing open spaces.

Under the cover of night, Bog moved into the campground, this time especially careful where and how he placed each step.

So far, so good.

After a few steps, Piney whispered from his shoulder, "Murky footprint. Looks like yours."

"It sure does," Bog said. "Everyone must've missed it in all the chaos."

He poured a small trickle of water onto the muddy print and gently swiped back and forth with the fern. "There. Now it's just... mud."

They worked slowly, retracing every step from the night before, undoing what had been done.

Bog took a deep sniff, and his eyes brightened. "I smell marshmallows!"

Piney yanked his ear. "Are you crazy?"

Bog's grin turned sly—very Vex-and-Hex.

"This is no time for Bigfoot jokes," Piney hissed. "Eyes down. Keep working."

Print by print, smear by smear, they erased the trail. Pride warmed Bog's chest as they slipped back toward the trees along the same hard spots they'd used to come in.

Just in time.

At the edge of the woods, Bog paused. Voices spilled from the campground's community building—a half dozen campers talking about a "monster" search party. Doors opened. Flashlights slashed the dark in jittery lines.

From the shadows, Bog spotted three deer and two opossums zigzagging across the grounds—careful and quiet—leaving green prints with every step.

One nudged a tipped bin upright. Another tugged a plastic bag from a shrub. Others scattered leaves over scuffs.

Word traveled fast in the woods.

Bog stifled a laugh. "They won't catch us tonight, Piney. Not tonight."

A faint radio crackle drifted from the service road. Piney's tail went still. "Ranger," he whispered.

CADAR
RIDGE
CAMPOUND

Chapter Four

"The Bigfoot Buzz"

News about a "possible" Bigfoot sighting spread fast at Cedar Ridge. By the time the sun ducked deep over the horizon, a group of campers had formed outside the community center—sleepy kids in pajama pants, dads with coffee, and more than a few phones held high.

Ranger Rudy eased his truck to the curb and rolled down the window. "What in the world are you all doing?" he asked, voice firm but steady. "Back from the road, please. Safety first."

He parked and stepped out, palms raised in a calm-down gesture. "Listen up. If you think you saw something, we're going to handle it the right way. No chasing through the woods, no splitting up, no drones."

Waldren lifted his phone like a trophy. "I have documented evidence—"

"You can show it to me," Rudy said, nodding toward the center. "Inside."

June slipped to his side. "Ranger, I can help," she said quickly. "If we bring folks in, I can do a Track ID mini-lesson—boots, deer, raccoon, beaver—so people know what they're looking at. Maybe you could add the safety part about not trampling nests or making casts in soupy mud?"

She was stalling... buying time for Bog.

Rudy studied her for half a beat, then gave a small, grateful smile. "Deal. Inside for cocoa and Track ID 101," he called to the crowd. "Phones away while we're learning."

Jinx groaned and jabbed a thumb toward the woods. "But the tracks—"

"Will still be there in fifteen minutes," Rudy said. "If they're real, they're not going anywhere."

Inside, June spread a tarp and laid out a few sheets of paper, a ruler, and a marker. "Okay, team," she said, her voice bright. "Who thinks a deer print looks like a heart? Who's seen raccoon hands? We'll draw, compare, and figure out what's what before anyone tromps the trails."

Kids crowded closer. Cocoa steamed. Waldren fidgeted but sat, clutching his phone under the table.

"And while we're at it," Rudy added, "Leave No Trace basics. Stay on paths. If you find something that looks important, don't step in it. Call me."

June caught a flicker at the window—a tiny black-and-white face. Penny Ping tapped the glass with her beak, then darted away toward the lake path.

June's stomach flipped. "Two minutes," she whispered to Rudy. "I'll grab a prop."

He nodded, trusting her.

She slipped toward the door, a plan forming. If Penny was flagging the lake, Bog might need a diversion.

I need Vex and Hex, June thought.

The two scampering scavengers were never far from a crowd. Part curious critter, part troublemaker, they watched from a nearby oak as the clutch of campers formed.

The campers spilled out of the community center like beans from a bag—no line, no plan. Then came Ranger Rudy and a bit behind, June.

Keeping a comfortable distance behind Rudy, June scanned the shadows for any sign of Vex and Hex.

It didn't take long. Soft chittering drifted toward her, then two striped tails. The raccoons hugged the edge of the light.

"I think Bog's on the lake trail," June whispered. "We need the crowd to head toward Willow Canyon instead."

Vex and Hex bobbed like nervous birds, then nodded. They had a plan.

Vex darted to the bulletin board and yanked down a faded "WILLOW CANYON LOOP" map with both paws.

He held it above his head like treasure and scampered three steps into the open.

Hex, all business, trotted to the garden hose, twisted the spigot with nimble fingers, and let a thin ribbon of water curl across the path—just enough to gleam in flashlight beams and start a muddy mess.

The kind that leaves muddy human prints everywhere they walked.

"Hey!" Jinx pointed. "Raccoons stole a map! And the trail is all wet!"

Hex and Vex were crafters of chaos.

Waldren swung his camera toward Willow Canyon as Vex waddled that way, map flapping dramatically. Flashlights followed the movement like moths.

Rudy raised his voice. "Stay together! No chasing wildlife—"

"Perfect!" June jumped in. "Willow Canyon has clear paths. Let's do a quick loop and compare tracks there—deer, fox, raccoon—then decide if we need to check the lake."

The group hesitated, then drifted after the map-waving raccoon. Hex killed the hose with a twist and vanished into the shrubs.

June caught Penny's flicker above the lake trail and exhaled. "Buy him thirty minutes," she whispered.

The group fell into a wobbly line and started down the Willow Canyon trail, flashlights wavering through the dark like a dozen fireflies.

Up front: Jinx and Waldren.

"Eyeshine!" Jinx yelped. "I saw eyeshine!"

Two hundred feet ahead, a towering oak hugged the trail. Eight feet up, Hex clung to the bark and leaned just far enough out for the beams to catch his eyes. When he ducked back, Vex leaned out from the other side.

Blink. Swap. Blink.

"It's a Bigfoot!" Jinx cried. "That's what they do—bob back and forth from behind trees!"

The crowd grew excited—too excited. Jinx and Waldren bolted toward the oak, phones up. They stopped fifteen feet from the trunk and swept their flashlights around the bark's edge.

"Nothing," Waldren said.

Jinx lifted his beam, lighting the trail another two hundred feet ahead. All of a sudden—blink. Swap. Blink.

"There!" Jinx shouted. "Up the trail—eyeshine again!"

By then, Ranger Rudy had reached the front. "Quiet," he said. "Everyone, quiet."

With the noise down, Vex and Hex slipped to the next tree without trouble. Vex began climbing the trunk when—

ker-thump! —a patch of bark gave way, and he tumbled to the ground. He and Hex darted off the trail, tails striping the dark.

"See?" Rudy said, pointing toward the rustle. "Raccoons. Keep beams low and stay on the path."

June knelt by the dirt at the trail's edge. "Check it out," she said, keeping her voice calm... and distracting. "Little hand prints—five fingers. Classic raccoon."

She peered into the dark where Hex and Vex had vanished. Smart little raccoons, she thought.

Up ahead, Waldren trudged with his face in his phone, thumbs flying.

"Posting raccoons now?" June said, dryly.

Waldren grumbled but kept tapping. "My fans like the material."

Ranger Rudy tried to organize the chaos into something less frightening than a Frankenstein posse. "Single file and calm," he called. "Keep your eyes peeled."

June fell back. With a flitter, Penny swooped to a nearby branch and gave one tweet.

Good. All clear, she thought. Bog and Piney must've made it past the lake to the relative safety of Shimmerleaf Hollow.

Rudy raised his voice just enough to gather the edges of the group. "Calm and steady. Eyes on the trail, not in the trees."

He glanced at his watch. "We'll finish the loop and call it a night."

June exhaled—then noticed Jinx bumping Waldren's elbow. The phone wobbled, camera swinging toward the lake as if directing him.

"Careful," June said, her tone easy but warning threaded through it. "Watch the roots."

Waldren huffed and righted his phone. "I've got it."

"Eyes on the ground," Rudy called. "We don't need any injuries."

June seized the moment. "Hey, track team—check this out." She knelt beside a bare patch of ground and traced the outline of a tiny track. "Rabbit. Sets of three. See? And here"—she pointed to a heart-shaped mark—"deer. If you look for these first, you won't miss what's real.

The line bunched, then smoothed again, attention pulled down to the earth instead of back toward the lake trail. Flashlights dipped. Voices softened into muttering.

They reached the trail head ten minutes later. Rudy turned to the group. "Thanks for keeping it calm, folks. We'll check the lake in daylight—fewer lights and more sense. For tonight: back to beds and cabins."

Groans sprinkled the crowd, but feet shuffled toward the glow of the community center.

Waldren lagged, tapping at his screen. "Mysterious eyes in Willow Canyon," he muttered, satisfied. "A teaser."

"Catchy," June said. "Accurate, too."

She hadn't meant to say the last part out loud.

He narrowed his eyes, not sure if she was teasing, then pocketed the phone and trudged after the others.

Outside, the night settled. June let out a slow breath and lifted two fingers to her lips. A soft, rising whistle—just once.

From deep in the trees, the answer came back, low and warm.

She smiled. Bog was safe.

Tomorrow, the rumor would still be there. So would Ranger Rudy's questions.

But for tonight, Cedar Ridge was quiet—and June had a plan.

Rudy lingered at the trail head, thumb on his radio. "First light, we check the lake—fresh prints, slow steps, bring plaster," he murmured, eyes drifting toward the dark water.

CANOE RACE
RESCHEDULED

Chapter Five

"The Big Letdown"

It was a new day in Cedar Ridge. June was curious—if a little nervous—about what it might bring. Bog was safe for now, but Waldren had posted pictures online—the kind that drew attention to Bigfoots.

She wasn't far from her tent when she heard Jinx's unmistakable snort.

"Ah-ha!" he crowed at Waldren. "Look at all these comments."

Waldren scrolled, frowning. One fellow cryptid vlogger had written, "Great eyeshine—now go get yours checked." Another asked, "Is that a mud print or a mud pie?"

June didn't enjoy anyone getting dunked on, but she couldn't help noting the upside: if people treated the post like a joke, it might take some pressure off Ranger Rudy.

Rudy stepped out of the community center with two steaming cocoas and handed one to June. "Crowd's thinner this morning," he said. "Looks like last night's excitement is turning into campfire stories."

"Good," June said, watching Waldren pocket his phone. "Stories are safer than search parties."

Rudy nodded. "I'm walking the lake trail after breakfast. You want to help with a track station for the younger campers?"

June smiled. "I've got a lesson ready."

Penny Ping zipped past overhead, a quick check mark in the sky. June relaxed. For now, at least, Cedar Ridge was back to breathing easy.

• • •

Back in Shimmerleaf Hollow, the air felt tighter. Bog's father, Bramdol—Bram for short—wasn't letting him off with a simple warning.

Bram was easygoing most days, but he took the clan's safety seriously. He also cast a formidable figure, towering over the other Bigfoots.

Bog pushed his breakfast around his plate while Bram spoke—about printing where humans could see, about curiosity wandering too close to camp, about how one mistake could bring a crowd.

"Adventure's fine," Bram said, voice low. "But we choose it where the forest stays safe."

His hand softened on Bog's shoulder. "Nana Moss is waiting at the creek. You'll help her today. Green prints only. You aren't to leave the hollow today."

Bog nodded, throat tight.

Piney squeezed his ear. "Status: grounded-but-okay," the squirrel whispered.

The young Bigfoot and his squirrel sidekick slunk from the table, eyes down, like they'd just eaten their last meal. Bog brimmed with adventure and curiosity, but disappointing his father knotted his stomach.

The path to Nana Moss's den usually took a minute; today it took ten—his big, furry-snowshoe feet shuffling through the leaves, slow as apology.

At the creek bend, Nana Moss's doorway of woven vines came into view. A curl of cedar-sweet steam drifted out.

"Two slow steps," Nana called without looking up. "That sounds like my Bogden—and a worried squirrel."

Piney gulped. "Status: extremely worried," he whispered.

Nana's eyes crinkled as they reached the threshold. "Good. Worried means you're ready to listen." She tapped the rim of a wooden bucket. "We've got water to teach and adventures to mend."

"Today, Bogden, we're gathering brambleberries," Nana said. "They're perfectly in season. Nothing teaches caution like the thorns on a brambleberry bush."

Collecting brambleberries was hard work, but somehow Nana made it seem like a treat.

Besides, Bog thought, fresh brambleberries could only mean one thing: brambleberry pie.

• • •

Ranger Rudy, June, and a handful of kids crept down the lake trail like they were tiptoeing across wet paint.

"I've never seen so many prints," Rudy breathed. "Deer, raccoon, fox—maybe even otter. Like the whole forest clocked in for a night shift."

He pointed as he went. "See the heart shapes? That's deer. Little hands? Raccoon. These neat, eggy ovals—fox. And this slide mark? Otter showing off."

June kept her face neutral and her heart full. The animals had done their part.

Rudy glanced up the shoreline. "Let's get photos for the nature board," he said. "And then we'll let the mud rest."

• • •

Meanwhile, back in Shimmerleaf Hollow, Bog was busy picking berries.

"Ouch!" he yelped, jerking his hand back. He held up his finger to inspect the damage.

Nana Moss only smiled, amusement crinkling her eyes. She shook her head. "Oh, child. The way of the woods is patience. Every move should be intentional—even your curious ones."

She guided his hand. "Back of the fingers first to part the thorns, then a gentle twist on the ripe berry. No grabbing, no rushing."

Piney peered from Bog's shoulder. "Status: poked," he whispered, then added, "Proceed with caution."

Bog tried again, slower this time. The berry came free with a soft pop. "Huh," he said, surprised.

Nana nodded. "Careful hands leave fewer scratches—and better stories."

She snipped a thorn with her thumbnail and sighed. "You know, Bog—I printed once."

Bog looked up.

"I was a young Bigfoot then. Younger than you. I was carefree and full of curiosity, always into something… just like you."

She nudged a bramble aside. "A family was packing up their campsite. They had a little girl—about June's age—who left her baby doll behind.

I wanted that doll so badly." Nana smiled at the memory, then shook her head. "I took it. But it wasn't mine."

Her eyes went distant. "That doll meant the world to that child. When they came back to look, they saw my tracks and followed them—almost to Shimmerleaf Hollow. Almost to our people."

She met Bog's eyes. "We mustn't take what isn't ours, Bogden. And we mustn't leave anything behind that tells the world we were here."

She tapped his knuckles lightly, guiding his hand past a thorn. "That's the code. If we make a mark, we fix it. If we take a thing, we give two back."

Bog swallowed. "What happened to the doll?"

"I put it where they'd find it and swept my prints until the forest forgot," Nana said. "I left a braid of sweet grass, too. A thank-you for the lesson." She smiled. "Now—back of the fingers, gentle twist. Try again."

• • •

June and Ranger Rudy cataloged and photographed a half dozen different animal signs along the lake trail.

"The sun's getting high," Rudy said, checking the light through the trees. "I bet these kids are ready for lunch. Let's head back."

They turned toward camp with Rudy leading and June bringing up the rear.

As the group rounded the last bend, June spotted Waldren at a picnic table, shoulders slumped, eyes on his phone.

"This is a disaster," he groaned. "Everyone thinks I made it up."

When June approached, he held the screen toward her. "See?" The headline from the local paper blared: "The Hoax of Cedar Ridge Strikes Again."

"I know it's real," Waldren said, voice tight. "Why won't anyone believe me?"

June sat on the bench's edge. "Sometimes believing isn't about proving," she said gently. "Sometimes the world's better with mysteries."

Rudy stopped beside them, setting a hand on the table. "And sometimes," he added, "we let the forest keep its own pace. Facts or fun, we treat this place with care."

Waldren swallowed and lowered the phone. Around them, kids laughed as they headed for the mess hall. Penny Ping zipped across the open space, a quick status check that eased June's mind about her furry friends.

June breathed a little easier.

"If you want," she offered, "you could help with the nature board. Real tracks. Real names. It's good work."

He hesitated, then nodded—seeds for future cooperation.

"Let's grab some lunch, Waldren, and talk about how we can help Cedar Ridge," June said.

Waldren stared at his phone a second longer, then slid it into his pocket. "Like... how?"

"Real tracks on the nature board," June said. "Leave No Trace tips. Maybe a Track ID walk that doesn't chase anything." She gave a half smile. "You'd be good at the mapping part."

Rudy nodded. "I could use helpers who care. Cameras down during lessons, though."

Jinx sauntered by with a tray, inviting himself. "As long as lunch is first," he said, already chewing.

They headed toward the mess hall together. Camp chatter rose—clatter, laughter, cocoa steam. For the first time all morning, Waldren's shoulders lifted.

At the doorway, June paused. Somewhere beyond the lake trail, a soft, familiar whistle drifted along the breeze— one note, warm and low.

She smiled to herself. "After lunch," she murmured. "Then we make a plan."

• • •

From the dark shadow of the pines among the brambleberries, Bog smiled. All seemed okay.

Rudy's radio crackled. "Gatehouse to Ranger—two vans just checked in asking about 'Bigfoot tours.' Out-of-state plates." He sighed, eyes lifting to the tree line. "Copy. We'll steer them to the bird walk—and keep eyes open this afternoon."

Rudy keyed the mike again. "And don't let the tourists hit the trails alone," "That's all we need is a stampede in Cedar Ridge."

Ranger Rudy paused, as if frozen, staring at the ground like he was puzzled by a line of ants.

June noticed too. The Ranger's gaze was momentarily frozen as if he was mentally checking out long enough to formulate a plan.

Chapter Six

"Back to Normal"

In the Cedar Ridge woods, things had almost returned to normal, save for a few extra tourists. A brand-new day was at hand, and Bog's trail suspension had been lifted—with stipulations.

Sunlight peeked through the cave entrance. Bog woke, stretched, and sat up on the pine-needle bed. "What adventure today, Piney?"

"Status: normal," squeaked the squirrel. "Lake trail is clear."

"Great idea, Piney. The lake it is!" Bog said, matter-of-fact. He'd only been grounded for a day, but excitement fizzed in his chest like Christmas morning.

He barely touched his nut-and-oat cereal before scooting his bowl aside. "May I be excused?"

Maple looked over from the hearth. "Where are you off to today, Bog?" she asked, though she clearly knew.

"Piney and I might do some fishing," Bog said, trying not to grin too big.

"And what is near the lake shore, Bog?"

"Mud."

"Keep your big feet out of it."

She had barely finished the sentence before Bog and Piney were out the door.

On the trail, Bog spotted Penny zipping overhead—almost certainly on orders from his mom and dad. One sharp chirp: all clear ahead.

The campground buzzed—not in a bad way, just busy. Unbeknownst to Bog, the young campers were getting ready for the annual canoe race across the lake, followed by a short hike up Thunder Ridge, where the winners would plant their flag. The camp was just big enough for two teams, four canoes each.

June wore red. Jinx wore blue.

This should be interesting, June thought.

Bog and Piney approached the bluffs rising some fifty feet above the south end of the lake.

Penny looped once over the boathouse, then arrowed back toward Bog—two chirps.

Piney shaded his eyes with a paw, squinting toward Penny. "Status: boats everywhere," he reported.

Bog grinned. "Adventure adjacent," he said. "Let's keep to the trees—and keep out of the mud."

. . .

Back at camp, the community center hummed with excited chatter as Ranger Rudy stepped to the front.

"Folks, listen up," he said in his best no-nonsense voice. "Today marks the tenth anniversary of the Camp Cedar Ridge woods race. To celebrate, we've got a special prize."

The room leaned in.

"Whoever paddles across the lake, hikes to Thunder Ridge, and plants their flag first," Rudy announced, "gets the other team to do their camp chores for two days."

The place exploded—cheers, groans, clattering benches.

Rudy raised a hand, smiling. "To keep it fair, I'll be stationed on Thunder Ridge to judge the finish. Counselors will accompany each canoe on the water and then bring up the rear on the trail. Safety first, teamwork always."

Jinx pumped a fist. June grinned at her team. Somewhere near the back, Waldren typed "Race Day!" into his phone and tried not to smile.

Kids poured out of the community center with the energy of an ant colony.

They clustered along the lake shore for last words before the start.

"Have a counselor check your safety gear, get into your canoe, and move to the start line," Ranger Rudy called through a megaphone. "Once everyone's lined up, we'll begin at the sound of my starter pistol."

Organizing a bunch of teenage campers was only slightly easier than herding cats. But at last, the canoes slid into place—reds on one side, blues on the other—paddles poised, life jackets snug, counselors ready.

June gripped the bow of a red canoe and flashed her team a grin. Across the line, Jinx bounced in his blue, already talking smack.

Out in the trees, a chickadee flicked past the shoreline. The lake went quiet, waiting.

Bang!

The canoes leaped forward. The experienced paddlers jumped to the lead, strokes snapping in sync, while others spun in wobbly circles, trying to make their paddles agree.

Rudy retreated to his old green truck and watched from the driver's seat for a moment. There was time. Even the fastest team would take two hours or more to reach Thunder Ridge.

He started the engine—squeak-squeak, rattle-rattle, vroom—and eased onto the logging road that wound toward the finish line. As the shoreline cheers faded behind him, the forest swallowed the sound of the race, leaving only the thrum of the truck and the promise of a flag waiting at the ridge.

On the lake, June settled into a steady rhythm. "Long pulls," she told her partner. Across the line, Jinx whooped and splashed, already dreaming of blue flags and no chores.

Bog and Piney, experts at hiding in plain sight, sat on the slate rock just beneath the cedars that lined the bluffs on the south end of the lake, watching the canoes race toward them. The takeout was only a hundred yards to the left, where the trail dipped to meet the water.

Laughter skimmed across the lake faster than the canoes. Paddle thumps echoed off the shore, closer with every heartbeat.

From a sun-warmed ledge, Bog and Piney shaded their eyes and watched the fleet glide in. Penny trilled once from above—hide now.

Bog nudged Piney deeper into the shadow of the trees as the first bow nosed past the reeds, kissing the shore where the trail met the water's edge. It was Jinx and his partner.

Oh no, June thought as her canoe slid in close behind. I'll never hear the end of his crowing.

One by one, fiberglass hulls hissed onto the sand at the foot of the trail. June didn't wait. With a red flag flapping from her backpack, she sprang up the path.

Jinx was fast, but he wasn't June on rough ground. She'd grown up in Cedar Ridge; these rocks knew her feet, and he was about to get schooled in hiking.

Bog and Piney held still as cattails waved in the soft lake breeze and counselors counted heads. Overhead, Penny circled once, then arrowed inland, trailing June's route toward the ridge. The climb pitched steep and rocky. June lengthened her stride. Just ahead, Jinx huffed and tried to keep the lead.

The bottleneck at the lake shore thinned as the racers spread into a line up the slope. From their rocky perch, Bog and Piney could just make out the bobbing red and blue helmets threading through the trees.

Farther back, the counselors spaced themselves along the trail, calling reminders and counting heads as the line climbed toward the ridge.

"This is the life, Piney," Bog said, almost reverent. With the disastrous days of accidental printing behind him, he let out a long, happy groan. "What do you think, my furry friend? Should we move closer to Thunder Ridge, catch the finish?"

Piney's ears perked. He nodded, and the two slipped deeper into the trees.

On the trail, the pack stretched out like an old slinky—long and loose—gaps opening between clusters of kids. The switchbacks tightened, one after another, making it harder for counselors to keep eyes on everyone as they called reminders around the bends.

About ten campers back from the lead, Robbie Odeham—Hammie to everyone—powered along. He was small for his age, but he made up for it with pure gusto. First into the pool, first to try the weird camp casserole, first to volunteer for anything. That's how the nickname stuck: Hammie always seemed to be showing off.

He adjusted his blue helmet and leaned into the next turn, eager to close the gap. Somewhere above, Penny's trill skimmed the treetops, and the line of red and blue bobbed higher toward the ridge.

With his head down, Hammie didn't realize his partner had outpaced him around the next tight turn.

"Skip! Wait up!" he called.

No response.

Eager to prove himself, Hammie picked up the pace, feet skittering over loose rock. The golden rule on rough ground was simple: know where each foot would land before it landed. Hammie wanted to catch his partner, and he broke the rule.

He was gaining... until disaster struck.

A tight corner lay ahead, where the trail switched back on itself and tree roots crossed like speed bumps. Hammie caught the toe of his boot on a root and lurched forward, off balance.

He windmilled once, missed the grab, and tumbled off the edge beside the trail—the steep side. The scream ripped across the canyon, bouncing from wall to wall until the hikers couldn't tell where it started.

Hammie had skidded off the trail and over the edge, clinging to a scrubby vine. His legs kicked for purchase, toes scraping air. Pebbles rattled loose and clacked down the slope to the hard, rocky ground thirty-five feet below.

Penny sliced overhead, firing a sharp string of chirps.

"Status—danger!" Piney gasped. "Someone's in trouble."

Bog didn't hesitate. He heard Nana's voice in his head: The code keeps us safe. Stay hidden. One exception—help anyone in danger.

With Piney clamped to his shoulder, Bog bolted toward the sound. Bigfoots weren't fooled by canyon echoes the way humans were.

Generations had taught them to read the forest: the way a cry bent around stone, the way birds lifted, the way branches told on the wind. Bog knew exactly where to go.

His long strides ate the ground in near silence, weaving through boulders and roots. In ten heartbeats, he reached the switchback and dropped into a crouch at the edge, eyes locking on the small blue helmet bobbing above.

"I see him," he breathed. "Hold on. We're gonna get you down."

• • •

Radios crackled to life as counselors shouted, "Emergency, emergency!"

Ranger Rudy had already heard the scream. The hikers were still a quarter mile from the finish, but the switchbacks put Rudy on a facing ridge, almost level with the spot where Hammie dangled.

He sprinted to a lookout and raised his binoculars. There—blue helmet, small hands clenched around a thin vine, feet kicking over empty air.

No way to reach him faster than the counselors on that side.

Rudy keyed his radio. "Thunder Ridge, this is Ranger Rudy. Stop all movement. Lead counselor, hold your position and keep the front group seated on the inside of the trail. Everyone else, reverse course now. You're past him—repeat, you're past him."

Static hissed, then confused replies. They'd already moved beyond the root where Hammie had tripped.

"Landmark check," Rudy said, voice steady. "You're looking for a tight right-hand switchback with a dead fall pine across the uphill side and a quartz outcrop on the corner. The victim is twenty feet below the bend. I have eyes on him."

"Copy," came a breathless answer. "Reversing. Counting heads."

"Good. One counselor stays with the lead. The rest move back with ropes if you have them. No runners. Slow and careful."

Across the gap, Rudy watched two red helmets begin to backtrack. He kept the binoculars fixed on Hammie and the radio pressed to his shoulder. "Hang on, kid," he murmured. "Help's coming."

"Come on, come on," Rudy muttered, breath tight. Through the binoculars, a swaying treetop snagged his attention. From his ridge, he could see only the canopy—a carpet of pine boughs hiding the ground below the young hiker. One trunk rocked harder, whipping side to side.

Crack—boom, the sound echoed throughout the canyon.

The tree toppled as if shoved by a bulldozer.

Rudy kept the lenses fixed on Hammie. The treetop rose into view beside the dangling boy, guided from below. Something—someone—was lifting it into place.

Down in the shadows, Bog braced his feet. He wasn't full-grown yet, but like any Bigfoot, he was strong—stronger than twenty men, Nana liked to say. He had rocked the tree, hugged it to wrench the roots free, and shouldered it to the cliff's edge.

"Grab the branches and climb down," he called up, steady and low.

Hammie clung to the vine with one hand and reached for a limb with the other. His boots found a solid branch. He let go of the vine and wrapped himself around the pine. Bog planted the base, angled the trunk against the rock, and held it fast.

"Climb down."

Panicked but moving, Hammie inched from branch to branch. Halfway to safety, he glanced toward the voice and caught a flash of fur and shadow as Bog slipped into the trees.

Across the canyon, Rudy's mouth fell open. A treetop had risen from the hidden forest and settled next to the boy; now the kid was climbing out of danger. When Hammie disappeared below Rudy's line of sight, counselors in red helmets finally appeared on the bend above.

"Did you see that?" Rudy blurted, forgetting to key his mic. He pressed the button and repeated, "Counselors on the switchback—did you see that tree move?"

"Negative," a voice crackled back. "No visual on the lower slope."

Rudy kept watching the place where the treetop had been, heart thudding. "Copy. Secure the rest of the hikers and hold your position. I'm climbing down to the canyon floor."

Chapter Seven

"Face-to-Face"

R udy's heart hammered as he pounded down a secondary trail to the canyon floor. He cut across a bed of soft pine needles and skidded to a stop.

Hammie sat on a rock beside the out-of-place pine, breathing fast but upright.

"Are you hurt, son?" Rudy called.

"I'm okay," the boy managed between quick breaths.

"What happened? What did you see?"

Hammie swallowed. "A giant, fur-covered man!" He pointed toward the trees.

Rudy turned his gaze to the forest. He took off his hat and scratched his head, more or less mumbling. "A big, hairy man, you say."

He keyed his mic. "Counselors, use the secondary trail to the canyon floor and bring the aid pack. I have the boy. He's stable."

"Copy," came the reply.

Rudy crouched beside Hammie, keeping his voice calm. "Robbie—Hammie—right? We're going to check you over. Any sharp pains? Dizziness?"

Hammie shook his head. "Just... scared."

"That's normal. You did great hanging on." Rudy angled a look at the leaning pine and the scuffed dirt where it had been dragged into place.

He'd seen the treetop rise. He just hadn't seen who—or what—had lifted it.

Footsteps and low voices scuffed closer. Counselors emerged from the trees with the aid pack, relief written all over their faces.

"Over here," Rudy said, standing and waving them in. "Let's do a quick assessment and get him hydrated. We'll debrief on the trail." He set his hat back on, eyes drifting once more to the quiet, shadowed forest. "And keep an eye out," he added softly. "For... anything."

Once Hammie was calm and steady on his feet, the group shouldered their packs and started up the secondary trail toward Thunder Ridge, Ranger Rudy bringing up the rear.

As he turned to follow, something snagged his eye—a dark tuft of fur caught in the thorns of a sticker bush, glinting in a shaft of sun.

Rudy stepped closer. He glanced up the trail to be sure no one was looking, then pinched the clump free and slipped it into his pocket without a word.

"Let's keep it moving," he called, voice even. But his hand stayed in his pocket, and his mind stayed on the shadowed trees below.

They topped out on the secondary trail and looked across to the finish. A speckled crowd of wood racers milled around the flag post, red and blue helmets bobbing. As soon as they spotted Hammie, kids pointed and shouted, "He's okay!"

Rudy lifted his hands for calm as they approached. "Look, folks, it's been an exciting day," he called, voice steady. "To be fair to everyone, we're postponing the race and redoing it tomorrow."

Groans rippled through the crowd, but most heads nodded. Deep down, they understood. No one looked more relieved than Jinx, who had been overtaken by curly-haired June shortly after the first ridge.

"Here's the plan," Rudy said. "Gather your gear and your thoughts. I'll shuttle you back to camp in groups of six in the truck bed. The rest of you start down the logging road with your counselors—slow and steady.

We'll leapfrog until everyone's back. Hydrate, stay with your buddy, and keep to the inside of the trail." The chatter softened into motion.

June squeezed Hammie's shoulder as she passed. Jinx stuffed his hands in his pockets and tried not to look too happy about a do-over. Above them, the ridge went quiet again, as if the trees were listening.

Bog and Piney crouched behind the wide stump of a walnut tree, watching the crowd gather, then thin, and finally disappear down the trail.

"Status update," Piney whispered. "Quiet now. We were seen."

"You don't know that," Bog said—though he didn't quite believe it himself.

Penny swept overhead and gave a single chirp.

"All clear for now," Piney translated.

"It's been an exciting morning," Bog said, letting out a breath of relief he'd been holding in. "Let's head for Shimmerleaf Hollow... by way of the blackberry patch."

Piney's whiskers twitched. "Mission-critical detour?"

"Absolutely," Bog said, already picturing purple-stained paws.

They slipped into the trees, keeping to the shadows as the ridge settled back into birdsong. Far above, Penny carved a lazy circle, then tilted her wings toward home.

. . .

Back at camp, news traveled fast—thanks in no small part to Waldren. Excited parents were already starting to fill the community center before Rudy pulled in with the last load of weary campers.

"Oh, brother," Rudy thought, "this is all we need."

He let out a long sigh, tipped his hat, and pushed open the community center door. The noise hit him like a wave—voices tumbling over one another, all asking the same thing: "What about the monster, Ranger?"

He raised both hands. "Folks, let's simmer down and take this one at a time."

The room quieted by inches.

"First, everyone is safe," he said. "Robbie—Hammie—is back with his counselors and doing fine. They're just checking him out as a precaution. We postponed the race and will rerun it tomorrow."

Murmurs steadied into a low buzz.

"As for what happened on Thunder Ridge," Rudy continued, choosing each word, "we're going to stick to facts. There was a fall. Counselors responded. The boy got down safely. Some said they heard echoes. Some said they saw movement in the trees." He paused. "We'll review what the staff observed and file a full safety report before we make any claims. In the meantime, there's no cause for panic."

A hand shot up. "But the monster—"

"We don't use that word," Rudy said gently. "If there's wildlife in the area, we'll identify it and adjust safety protocols. Until then, let's focus on looking out for each other."

He tipped his hat again. "Counselors will have updated schedules in the morning. Relax, eat dinner, and rest up for tomorrow."

As the crowd slowly broke into smaller groups of chatter, Rudy slid his hand into his pocket and felt the soft tuft of fur. He kept his face calm, but his eyes drifted to the window, out toward the dark edge of the woods.

Thanks to Waldren's website, news of a possible "furry man-beast" sighting had already leaked beyond camp. A dirty old pickup rattled along the service road behind the campsites, keeping out of sight. This wasn't part of the regular crowd.

The driver was Charles Cormier—Charlie to most—local "cryptid photographer." He made his living selling blurry pictures to small-town papers and anyone who liked a good scare. To Bog, he was trouble with a capital T.

The truck squeaked to a stop, throwing a plume of dust across the sun baked trail. Charlie grinned at the empty woods. "Got you now," he muttered.

Without taking his beady eyes off the tree line, he slid out the driver's door and moved to the tailgate. He dropped it with a clank and peeled back a small blanket, slow as if he were lifting the lid on a steaming pizza.

Underneath sat a brand-new drone. Sleek. Mean. Wired with an infrared camera set to chase and snap pictures of any large heat signature it found.

The kind of heat a Bigfoot might create.

.....

Back at the blackberry patch, Bog and Piney were having a time. Black-blue smears stained big paws and small paws alike. They chomped sweet berries two at a time, nearly missing Penny as she knifed a sharp loop overhead.

Two sharp chirps.

"Danger, danger," Piney chittered, fur bristling. He squinted up. "Wait—giant mosquito? That can't be right."

"You're berry-drunk, Piney," Bog grinned.

Beyond the tree line, a loud buzz shouldered into the quiet. It slid left to right—buzzz—growing, fading, growing again.

Penny sliced low. Another double chirp. Urgent.

"What is that, Piney?" Bog hissed.

They didn't wait to find out. Strange noises usually meant humans—and trouble. Piney clenched Bog's shoulder fur as Bog loped for the deeper woods.

The buzz fell away behind them. They stopped, catching their breath.

It returned, louder.

Bog took off again, faster. The wind tugged Piney's ears flat. The faster Bog ran, the louder the buzz swelled—now a snarl.

They broke toward Shimmerleaf Hollow. One small meadow lay ahead, bright with late evening sun.

Bog skidded to a stop at the edge so hard Piney nearly tumbled free.

There, hovering at eye level above the grass, was the biggest "mosquito" Bog had ever seen. It hung on four spinning wings and stared with one shiny, glassy eye. A red dot winked.

A white-hot flash, like lightning, cracked the clearing.

Bog threw his arm up, covering his eyes. Spots danced in his vision.

"Downhill—into the thicket!" Piney hissed.

Bog lunged down slope. Branches slapped and snagged; the machine dived after them, then jerked back from the tangle with an angry whine.

They plunged into a green knot of alders and thorns and went still. Shimmer, breathe, vanish.

Above the brambles, the red eye drifted, still searching for a heat signature.

Piney squeezed his eyes closed, so did Bog. Thoughts of shimmer, breathe, vanish rolling across their minds like a memory, both secretly wishing and wanting for the safety of Shimmerleaf hollow in that very moment.

That's the end of this adventure for now. Be sure to find out how our friends fool the metal mosquito in

The Bigfoot of Cedar Ridge

The Adventures of Bog Book 2

"Escape from Cedar Ridge"

Other Works by these Authors

on Squatchcamppress.com and other fine literary retailers

The Space Between Thoughts (early 2026)
From visionary leader, licensed therapist, and PhD, Dr. Ravenlight—lifelong empath and Medium—*The Space Between Thoughts* blends grounded insight with poetic, soulful guidance to help you unlock intuition, read energy, and return to calm, aligned presence. Through 25 luminous chapters, it invites you to release performance, protect your peace, and embody your power from a place of quiet inner knowing.

Tarot Decks by Dr. Suzzanna Ravenlight (early 2026)
Combining over 25 years of leadership and organizational change with a lifetime as a Medium and Empath, Dr. Suzzanna Ravenlight brings to you her magical and inspirational tarot and oracle decks.

The Bigfoot of Cedar Ridge: The Adventures of Bog – Book One "Footprint Fiasco"
In *Foot Print Fiasco*, Robert Rogers introduces Bog, a snack-loving thirteen-year-old Bigfoot, and Piney, his rule-narrating fox squirrel sidekick, as they scramble to erase a muddy mistake before Ranger Rudy discovers the truth. Packed with humor, heart, and a dash of mystery, this adventure celebrates friendship, courage, and keeping secrets when it matters most.

The Bigfoot of Cedar Ridge: The Adventures of Bog – Book Two "Escape from Cedar Ridge"
In Robert Rogers's *Escape from Cedar Ridge*, Bog must protect his hidden clan when a heat-seeking drone invades the ancient Veil Path and pulls determined kids deeper into the forest's secrets. As myth collides with modern tech, Bog

may have to break the oldest rule of all to keep his family safe.

The Bigfoot of Cedar Ridge: The Adventures of Bog – Book Three "Friend or Foe" (late 2025)
In Book Three of the Bigfoot of Cedar Ridge series, Robert Rogers invites you to come along with our furry Bigfoot friends as they discover who knows the secrets of Cedar Ridge, and who is willing to keep them, out in late 2025.

The Healthcare Wars: "Rise of the Resistance" (early 2026)
In the long-awaited sequel to The Healthcare Wars: Maximum Resistance, a machine-run regime called F.A.I.T.H. controls who receives care—and who gets erased—until an underground network of medics, hackers, and soldiers strikes back from the shadows. As the system adapts and hunts them down, the Resistance fights to reclaim the basic right to live beyond the algorithm's judgment.